W9-BTM-410

THE LOG CABIN CHURCH

BY Ellen Howard
ILLUSTRATED BY Ronald Himler

HOLIDAY HOUSE / NEW YORK

Printed in the United States of America
www.holidayhouse.com
First Edition

Library of Congress Cataloging-in-Publication Data
Howard, Ellen.
The log cabin church / by Ellen Howard; illustrated by Ronald Himler.—1st ed.
p. cm.
Summary: On the Michigan frontier, while the adults disagree
over whether there are enough settlers yet to build a church,
a young girl tries to recall what church is all about.
ISBN 0-8234-1740-9
[1. Church—Fiction. 2. Frontier and pioneer life—Michigan—Fiction.
3. Family life—Michigan—Fiction. 4. Michigan—Fiction.]
I. Himler, Ronald, ill. II. Title.

PZ7.H82835 Lo 2002
[E]—dc21 2001059443

For Harper Quincannon,

from her granny

E. H.

To Claire Counihan

R. H.

“Come spring, we’ll see about buildin’ a church,” my pap had said at Christmastime.

It was certain that Granny wanted a church, but it set me to pondering hard. Seemed like I could scarcely bring to mind our church in Carolina. I recollected the churchyard, where we buried our mam. I recollected the preacher, black-clad and tall, at the side of the grave. I recollected the clods of dirt a-falling on the coffin. What did we need with a church?

"Tell me about church, Bub," I said to my brother.

He was chopping at a pine tree, and his ax thunked with his words.

"Church? Why, church is where you go Sabbaths, Elvirey," he said. He stopped to wipe his brow, and grinned. "To see the purty gals."

"There ain't no purty gals in Michigan," I said.

"What did we do at church, Sis?" I asked my sister.

She was kneeling by the thawing spring, scouring a kettle with sand.

"Why, we sang, Elvirey," Sis said. "It was grand to hear the folks sing praises to the Lord."

"We can do that without a church," I said. "We sang at Christmastime."

"Granny," I said one evening by the fire. "What's the use of a church?"

Granny humphed and rocked hard and shot a look at my pap.

"The child don't even know what a church is for," she said. "She's a-growin' up heathen out here in the wilds."

But she didn't tell me. I couldn't see why we needed a church.

Spring came to our Michigan woods. It came of a sudden when the snow was gone, popping out of the mud all green. The water commenced to gurgle. The trees was filled with birds.

Folks came, too. Their wagons rumbled on the trail. Younguns ran ahead, shouting. Mothers and babies jounced in the wagons. Men stopped to have a word with Pap. I saw a purty gal.

Times, we put up a family for the night. Times, Pap and Bub was called to pull a wagon from the mud. Times, Granny gave folks supper or a drink from our spring.

"Word is gettin' out," said Pap, "about this good new land."

"Now that folks is a-comin'," said Granny, "it's time to build a church."

But first, Pap said, it was time for clearing the field. There was a powerful lot of trees. Pap and Bub chopped. Sis and me grubbed brush. We burned logs and stumps 'til the air filled with smoke.

Still folks came. There commenced to be other clearings in the woods, and fires burned day and night.

"The church," Granny said.

But next it was time for plowing, Pap said. He followed along behind our old horse. I set on the plowshare to weight it to the ground and watched the soil turn up, all moist and black and deep.

We worked sunup to sundown.

"Not on the Sabbath!" Granny cried.

"Do you want to eat?" said Pap.

It was time for planting, Pap said. He got out the seed corn and wheat.

"This growin' is up to the Lord," said Granny when the seeds was in the ground. "It is time to build the church."

On a Sabbath morning, midsummer, we didn't go to the field. I could see that Pap was chafing, thinking of the weeds growing fast as the corn. But he washed his face and hands, and put on his Sunday coat. He made us younguns wash, too.

“Folks is a-comin’,” said Granny.

The Campbells came first, with the sun scarcely up.

Missus drove and Mister led the ox, and their passel of kids hung over the wagon sideboard, a-whooping!

Then Mr. Galloway and his young wife and Mrs. Galloway’s mam. Widow Aiken and her big tall boys. The Clabaughs and the Grays. The cabin filled up, and the corn cakes was et as fast as Granny could cook ’em. The women talked to make my ears ring.

The menfolk went outside.

I was set to mind the least ones. I played with the Campbell baby 'til Sis bore him away. I wiped the Clabaugh noses. I kept Junior Gray from falling in the spring.

Bub was making eyes at the purty Campbell gal.

Now and again, I listened to the men.

"There ain't enough folks yet to build a church," said Pap.

"Do you begrudge the Lord?" thundered Mr. Gray.

"Begrudgin' ain't nothing to do with it," yelled Pap.

"I reckon it might be sense to wait," said Mr. Galloway.

"Still an' all," said Mr. Campbell, "the womenfolk want a church now."

I slipped into the cabin, where the women was fixing dinner.

Sis rocked the Campbell baby in Granny's rocking chair. Mrs. Campbell told a story, and the cabin rang with laughter. Then Mrs. Galloway's mam was a-telling of their journey, and Mrs. Galloway commenced to weep.

"It's the child we buried alongside the road," said Mrs. Galloway's mam.

Widow Aiken bowed her head. Mrs. Gray passed a kerchief.

"I left two babes a-buried back home," whispered Mrs. Gray.

Seemed there was nothing more to say.

I thought to commence to sing as our mam used to sing.

"Blest be the tie that binds," I sang, 'til we all was singing, the womenfolk and gals, as we chopped and stirred and fried the meat.

Dinnertime, we carried out the food to the rugs and quilts we'd spread on the ground. Granny sent me to fetch the menfolk.

They was talking, quietlike. I saw Mr. Gray put his hand on Pap's shoulder as they shuffled over to eat.

Granny gave Pap a look. He bowed his head.

"Brothers and sisters," he said, "let us pray."

I bowed down my head, but I peeked. The younguns was wiggling, a-smelling the food. The women was smooth-faced and peaceful. Even the men seemed calm.

I wondered if we would build a church right soon. But it didn't seem to matter.

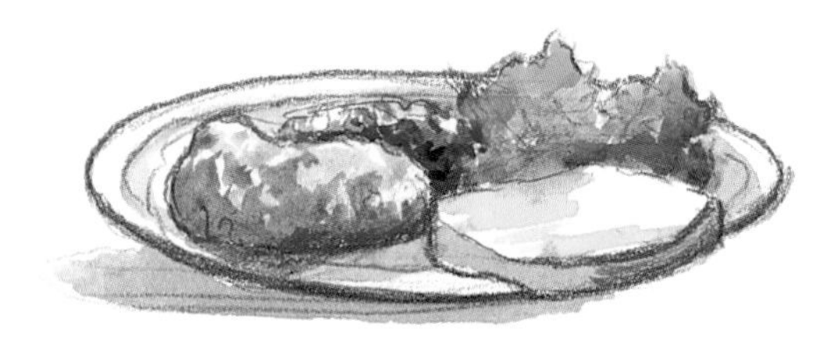

As I looked at their faces, it come to me. I could recollect church back home.

There had been boys and gals a-courting. There had been talking and singing and praying. There had been joy and sorrow and comfort. There had been neighbors.

Like in our cabin that day.